W9-AAZ-426

Alexander and the Terrible, Horrible, No Good, Very Bad Day

JUDITH VIORST

Illustrated by RAY CRUZ

Aladdin Books
Macmillan Publishing Company
New York

Aladdin Books
Macmillan Publishing Company
866 Third Avenue, New York, NY 10022
Collier Macmillan Canada, Inc.

Second Aladdin Books edition 1987
Printed in the United States of America

A hardcover edition of *Alexander and the Terrible, Horrible, No Good, Very Bad Day* is available from Atheneum Publishers, Macmillan Publishing Company

10 9 8 7 6

Library of Congress Cataloging-in-Publication Data
Viorst, Judith.
Alexander and the terrible, horrible, no good, very bad day.
Summary: One day when everything goes wrong for him, Alexander is consoled by the thought that other people have bad days too.
[1. Humorous stories] I. Cruz, Ray, ill. II. Title.
PZ7.V816A1 1987 [E] 87-1087
ISBN 0-689-71173-5 (pbk.)

For Robert Lescher, with love and thanks

I went to sleep with gum in my mouth and now there's gum in my hair and when I got out of bed this morning I tripped on the skateboard and by mistake I dropped my sweater in the sink while the water was running and I could tell it was going to be a terrible, horrible, no good, very bad day.

At breakfast Anthony found a Corvette Sting Ray car kit in his breakfast cereal box and Nick found a Junior Undercover Agent code ring in his breakfast cereal box but in my breakfast cereal box all I found was breakfast cereal.

I think I'll move to Australia.

In the car pool Mrs. Gibson let Becky have a seat by the window. Audrey and Elliott got seats by the window too. I said I was being scrunched. I said I was being smushed. I said, if I don't get a seat by the window I am going to be carsick. No one even answered.

I could tell it was going to be a terrible, horrible, no good, very bad day.

At school Mrs. Dickens liked Paul's picture of the sailboat better than my picture of the invisible castle.

At singing time she said I sang too loud. At counting time she said I left out sixteen. Who needs sixteen?
I could tell it was going to be a terrible, horrible, no good, very bad day.

I could tell because Paul said I wasn't his best friend anymore. He said that Philip Parker was his best friend and that Albert Moyo was his next best friend and that I was only his third best friend.

I hope you sit on a tack, I said to Paul. I hope the next time you get a double-decker strawberry ice-cream cone the ice cream part falls off the cone part and lands in Australia.

There were two cupcakes in Philip Parker's lunch bag and Albert got a Hershey bar with almonds and Paul's mother gave him a piece of jelly roll that had little coconut sprinkles on the top. Guess whose mother forgot to put in dessert?

It was a terrible, horrible, no good, very bad day.

That's what it was, because after school my mom took us all to the dentist and Dr. Fields found a cavity just in me. Come back next week and I'll fix it, said Dr. Fields.

Next week, I said,
I'm going to Australia.

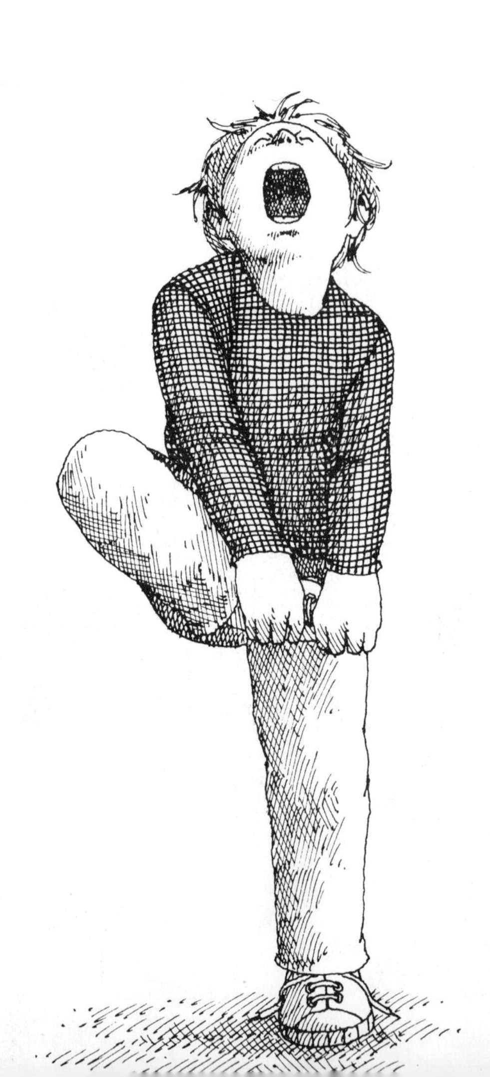

On the way downstairs the elevator door closed on my foot and while we were waiting for my mom to go get the car Anthony made me fall where it was muddy and then when I started crying because of the mud Nick said I was a crybaby and

661

while I was punching Nick for saying crybaby my mom came back with the car and scolded me for being muddy and fighting.

I am having a terrible, horrible, no good, very bad day, I told everybody. No one even answered.

So then we went to the shoestore to buy some sneakers. Anthony chose white ones with blue stripes. Nick chose red ones with white stripes. I chose blue ones with red stripes but then the shoe man said, We're all sold out. They made me buy plain old white ones, but they can't make me wear them.

When we picked up my dad at his office he said I couldn't play with his copying machine, but I forgot. He also said to watch out for the books on his desk, and I was careful as could be except for my elbow. He also said don't fool around with his phone, but I think I called Australia. My dad said please don't pick him up anymore.

It was a terrible, horrible, no good, very bad day.

There were lima beans for dinner and I hate limas.

There was kissing on TV and I hate kissing.

My bath was too hot, I got soap in my eyes, my marble went down the drain, and I had to wear my railroad-train pajamas. I hate my railroad-train pajamas.

When I went to bed Nick took back the pillow he said I could keep and the Mickey Mouse night light burned out and I bit my tongue.

The cat wants to sleep with Anthony, not with me.

It has been a terrible, horrible, no good, very bad day.

My mom says some days are like that.

ECOLOGY
POWER!

Even in Australia.